Samuel French Acting Edition

Queen

W9-CCY-676

by Madhuri Shekar

‖SAMUEL FRENCH‖

be invented, including mechanical, electronic, photocopying, recording, videotaping, or otherwise, without the prior written permission of the publisher. No one shall upload this title(s), or part of this title(s), to any social media websites.

For all enquiries regarding motion picture, television, and other media rights, please contact Concord Theatricals Corp.

MUSIC USE NOTE

Licensees are solely responsible for obtaining formal written permission from copyright owners to use copyrighted music in the performance of this play and are strongly cautioned to do so. If no such permission is obtained by the licensee, then the licensee must use only original music that the licensee owns and controls. Licensees are solely responsible and liable for all music clearances and shall indemnify the copyright owners of the play(s) and their licensing agent, Concord Theatricals Corp., against any costs, expenses, losses and liabilities arising from the use of music by licensees. Please contact the appropriate music licensing authority in your territory for the rights to any incidental music.

IMPORTANT BILLING AND CREDIT REQUIREMENTS

If you have obtained performance rights to this title, please refer to your licensing agreement for important billing and credit requirements.

QUEEN was first produced by Victory Gardens (Chay Yew, Artistic Director; Erica Daniels, Executive Director) in Chicago, Illinois on April 14, 2017. The performance was directed by Joanie Schultz, with sets by Chelsea M. Warren, costumes by Janice Pytel, lights by Heather Gilbert, sound and original music by Thomas Dixon, projections by Aaron Quick, and dramaturgy by Isaac Gomez. The production stage manager was Lynne M. Harris. The cast was as follows.

SANAM SHAH . . . . Priya Mohanty

ARIEL SPIEGEL . . . . .Darci Nalepa

ARVIND PATEL. . . . . .Adam Poss

DR. PHILIP HAYES. . . . . Stephen Spencer

CHARACTERS

SANAM SHAH – (29-30) F. Indian (from India – accented speech.) An applied mathematician about to graduate from a Ph.D. program in ecology.

ARIEL SPIEGEL – (33-34) F. White. A Ph.D. ecology researcher and single mom.

ARVIND PATEL – (Late 30s) M. Indian-American. A financier from New York. A potential suitor for Sanam.

DR. PHILIP HAYES – (Late 40s-Early 50s) M. White. Ariel and Sanam's supervising professor.

SETTING

Santa Cruz, California

TIME

2016

Scene One

(An outdoor happy hour.)

*(**SANAM** and **ARIEL** sit at a table, drinking beer.)*

ARIEL. I think I need to find a new day care.

SANAM. Why? I thought you liked them.

ARIEL. They're calling me now to tell me that Rissi is biting the other kids. Biting! Like my daughter is some kind of feral wolf child. Can you imagine Rissi even hitting another kid, or pinching them, or whatever? Something weird must have gone down and now they're blaming it on her. They've sent me a list of resources. Resources!

SANAM. Oh, Rissi bites.

ARIEL. What?

SANAM. She bit me once. When I was baby-sitting.

ARIEL. What? When did this happen?

SANAM. Uh, like a month ago. Bit my cheek. Right here.

ARIEL. What? Why didn't you say anything?

SANAM. It was cute. She is a feral wolf child sometimes.

ARIEL. Dear god. My daughter is a...a...predator!

I can't believe I have to take a two year old to therapy now.

*(**SANAM** tsks.)*

SANAM. You don't need therapy and all that. Just bite her back.

ARIEL. What?

SANAM. That way she knows it's bad.

ARIEL. Sanam.

SANAM. It's a scientific principle. Cause and effect. You bite someone, it hurts.

ARIEL. Weirdo. I'm not gonna bite my kid.

(*Looking around.*)

Who are all these people?

SANAM. Ph.D. students, post-docs, professors...who else would be here?

ARIEL. I know that. But they're not from our lab.

SANAM. They've heard about the spectacular happy hours that we organize. Our happy hours actually have ice. And beer. That's two huge things in our favor.

ARIEL. I'm not organizing these stupid things anymore. Nowhere in my job description, nowhere in my student funding, does it say that I need to organize happy hours.

SANAM. But if you don't do it, it won't happen.

ARIEL. I know. That's my curse. I just have to...take care of everything.

(*Nudging* **SANAM.**)

Cute Indian nerd. Three o'clock.

SANAM. Stop pointing out every Indian nerd to me.

ARIEL. Sorry. I thought that was our thing.

SANAM. My parents are setting me up again.

ARIEL. Again?

SANAM. Yes. Again. I'm not married yet, am I? So yes, they'll keep setting me up. I'm meeting him next Thursday, I think. They're so excited about this one. His grandfather played golf with my grandfather.

ARIEL. I keep forgetting you're rich.

SANAM. I'm not rich.

ARIEL. Compared to how I grew up?

SANAM. I'm not rich. My parents are rich. I'm surviving on beef jerky and beer.

ARIEL. Anyway. What's this guy like?

SANAM. No clue.

He works for a trading firm...or something...on Wall Street.

ARIEL. Um, ew. Do not meet him.

SANAM. He lives in New York. Financial district. In a Trump building.

ARIEL. Ewww. Don't meet him.

SANAM. I have to.

ARIEL. Fine. I give you permission to sleep with him once and then break his heart.

SANAM. I'm not doing that! I'd never be attracted to someone my parents selected for me. Would you?

ARIEL. Ugh. No. You're right. Okay, so what do you want? Why do you keep going on these dates?

SANAM. You know what I do want?

I want to be like Shakuntala Devi.

ARIEL. That Indian math genius, right?

SANAM. Yes. They called her the human calculator. She could calculate the twenty-third root of a two hundred digit number all in her head. She was born in 1929 and despite being a woman, she became one of the greatest, most influential mathematicians India's ever produced.

ARIEL. You're kind of like her. You're practically there already.

SANAM. One thing most people don't know about her is that her husband was gay.

ARIEL. Really?

SANAM. Yeah. They had this really great marriage because he was gay, and she was a career woman. So that's what I want.

ARIEL. A...gay husband?

SANAM. Yes!

That way I get my parents off my back, and I get to do whatever I want.

Think of everything I could accomplish if I had a gay husband who would happily leave me alone!

ARIEL. *(Pause.)* I wish I were gay.

>   (**SANAM** *shoots her a look.* **ARIEL** *shoots one back. They make silly faces at each other. They drink.)*

SANAM. Look, there's that guy you made out with at trivia night.

ARIEL. Yeah...

SANAM. Not gonna talk to him?

ARIEL. Oh, we were getting along great. Didn't even mind the whole single mom thing. Then he found out that you and I were getting published in *Nature.*

SANAM. So?

ARIEL. *(Loving this.)* So he stopped texting. It was like, so obvious, it was actually kind of funny. He's a post-doc, and he couldn't handle the fact that a mere Ph.D. student was getting published in motherfrickin' *Nature.*

SANAM. Seriously?

Wait.

Is that why everyone else has been ignoring us too?

ARIEL. Uh, yeah.

SANAM. No wonder nobody's coming over to talk to us. I thought I was just imagining things.

ARIEL. *(Gleeful.)* Oh no. Everyone hates us now. They're burning up with jealousy.

SANAM. It shouldn't be a competition.

ARIEL. But it is. And we won.

>   (**ARIEL** *clinks beers with* **SANAM.**)

SANAM. We're not published yet. We still have to present at the conference, and we have that final batch of field data to work on –

ARIEL. Yeah but those are just formalities. We're in. We're getting published in the most high-impact science journal in the world, and they can't stand it.

>   *(Pointing people out.)*

Look at Rosenfeld and her team. You almost joined that lab. Remember? In your first year? Look at Sloan, Pace, Menendez – you almost joined their labs. But no. You chose my project. And now you're getting published in *Nature*.

SANAM. Look at Rosenfeld and her team. I almost joined their lab. They almost got published in *Nature*. Sloan, Pace, Menendez, they almost got published in *Nature* too. But no. I chose your project. And now you're getting published in *Nature*.

ARIEL. Touché.

(They clink their beers again.)

SANAM. I should get going.

ARIEL. No, don't go. My mom has Rissi tonight. I can actually hang out.

SANAM. All this talk about the paper – I want to get home and keep working on that final data set.

ARIEL. Why?

SANAM. I'm having some trouble. I'm not getting the same results when I input the latest batch of field data.

ARIEL. Really?

SANAM. The undergrads must have screwed up the data entry, or something. I'm trying to find the bug, so that I can debug it.

ARIEL. Do you want to e-mail Philip?

SANAM. No. No. I'll fix this on my own.

ARIEL. He's our professor. I think he'd want to know. He's making the official announcement in like ten days.

SANAM. No, I don't want to bother him. He's getting ready for that conference in Sweden, and, and he'll just be weird about it right now –

ARIEL. Sanam, he actually likes you.

SANAM. No, he likes you.

ARIEL. If he's being weird, it's just because there's so much riding on this project, you know? You can't take it personally. This paper is his ticket to like, real money. Real influence. He's in talks with big industry players – he might be heading up a huge private lab in Boston.

SANAM. He's leaving the university?

ARIEL. That's what he told me.

SANAM. Okay. Well. This is exactly why I don't want to bother him. I'll just fix it. No big deal. I'll fix it. I always fix it.

(Transition to – .)

Scene Two

(**SANAM** *and* **ARIEL***'s shared office.*)

(**SANAM** *is at her computer, freaking out.*)

(**ARIEL** *enters with coffee.*)

SANAM. I can't fix it.

ARIEL. What?

SANAM. The new data set. I can't fix it. The results keep skewing in the wrong direction. I don't know what's going on.

ARIEL. Wait, what? I thought you were making progress.

SANAM. I scrubbed the field data clean, I even cross-checked the data points as much as I could – the new data set is throwing us off.

ARIEL. Why?

SANAM. I don't know. And he's coming back tomorrow. What am I going to say?

ARIEL. I'm sure everything is fine. And he might even be able to help us.

SANAM. I don't know.

ARIEL. And he just wants to see the presentation and the speech tomorrow. The actual submission deadline for the paper is still a month away. We have time.

SANAM. But we have to show our results in the presentation.

ARIEL. We can...put in our projections. Yeah. I mean, we know what the final results are going to be.

(**DR. PHILIP HAYES** *enters, dressed in a travel coat.*)

HAYES. How are my two favorite worker bees?

(*The* **WOMEN** *are shocked.*)

ARIEL. Philip!

SANAM. Dr. Hayes.

(**HAYES** *places a stuffed honey bee on the desk.*)

HAYES. Here you go. Compliments of the Scandinavian Ecological Society.

ARIEL. We weren't expecting you back today.

HAYES. Took an earlier flight.

We got some news.

ARIEL. What's that?

HAYES. It's happening in D.C. The bill's been revived. They're working on it as we speak.

> (**ARIEL** *is so shocked she just stares at him for a second.*)

ARIEL. THE bill? The Saving America's Pollinators Act of 2012? *Now* it gets revived? *Now?*

HAYES. Stranger things have happened.

ARIEL. I don't think they have. What changed?

> (**HAYES** *smiles. He's smug but he's earned it.*)

HAYES. We finally have proof.

ARIEL. …Our paper?

HAYES. Exactly. And it's not just any paper. It's being published by *Nature*. It's going to be on the cover. The NRDC took that to Congress, and they're finally starting to listen. And look, when it comes down to it, big agriculture will be decimated if the pollinators go extinct.

ARIEL. The commercial stakes are huge.

HAYES. Huge. So we have the right Congressmen willing to play ball, and the bill's back on the table.

ARIEL. Oh my god.

HAYES. I spoke to Spivak. You remember her, right? From the NRDC? They're going to be using our language – they're going to be *citing* our paper.

ARIEL. No. No way.

HAYES. Your names are going to be cited in the legislation that will finally ban the neonics in the United States.

(**ARIEL** *is momentarily at a loss. She looks around, excitement overwhelming her. She grabs a cushion and squeals into it.*)

SANAM. Very exciting.

(**ARIEL** *puts down the cushion.*)

ARIEL. Wow. Okay. Sorry about that. That's incredible, Philip. That's incredible.

HAYES. So it's more important than ever that we nail this on Monday – important people are going to be following this, real closely. So let's see it.
The speech. The presentation.

(*The* **WOMEN** *dart a look at each other.*)

ARIEL. Uh, your speech is ready, but the presentation –

HAYES. That's fine. Just show me what you have.

ARIEL. (*Grabbing her legal pad.*) Sanam, could you load it up?

(**SANAM** *types – worried – .*)

SANAM. Yes.

(**SANAM** *loads a presentation on her computer.*)

ARIEL. Here you go.

(*She hands* **HAYES** *the legal pad full of handwritten notes.*)

Sorry about my handwriting, I'll just tell you the speech.

(*She does the speech. She knows it.*)

"Ladies and gentlemen, I am Dr. Philip Hayes, and it is my honor to be here today, at the National Conference for the Ecological Society of America, accepting the 2016 George M. Moffet award in recognition of long-term contributions to ecological research. Thanks to the brilliant work of my two senior graduate students –"

HAYES. Oh really.

ARIEL. Yes, really. "– I stand before you today, proud to announce that our upcoming paper on the fundamental relationship between Neonicotinoid Pesticides and Colony Collapse Disorder will be published in the September first issue of *Nature*."

And then we pause for a round of applause, and watch the Stanford guys just, like, melt into a puddle of jealous...like, tears.

HAYES. Very good. Go on.

ARIEL. "For over a decade, the School of Environmental Science here at the University of Santa Cruz has toiled relentlessly to solve one of the most alarming ecological questions in our world today – why are the bees disappearing?

Not even dying, you see. Disappearing. We can't even find the bodies. Colony Collapse Disorder entails the disappearance of up to thirty percent of bee colonies around the world on an annual basis. And as we know, the human race simply cannot exist without honey bees. If we let CCD continue unabated, we can say goodbye to ninety percent of the food that we grow, to fruits and vegetables and basic nutrition.

But why is this happening? For years we've struggled to find the cause. Could it be climate change? Electromagnetic radiation? A bee virus, a mutation?

As it turns out, it was the dirty little secret we'd suspected all along, the thing that had been whispered about but never dare spoken aloud, that little voice in our heads saying...

Monsanto."

You know last night when I was putting Rissi to bed, I told her she needed to go to sleep right away or Monsanto would get her, and she was out like a light.

HAYES. *(Chuckling.)* Very good.

ARIEL. Okay, here's the rest.

    (Reading.)

"One pesticide – one pesticide – manufactured by this agricultural monolith has been responsible for wiping out seven billion bees over the past ten years.

(Meaningful pause.)

"The scientific community has suspected this for long, sure, we've suspected it, but we do not accuse without evidence. And finally, thanks to the pioneering work of our team here at UCSC, we have evidence.

(Excited, going off script a little.)

"And we are coming for Monsanto. Oh yes, the day of reckoning has arrived."

HAYES. Wow.

Good.

Very good.

*(**ARIEL** beams.)*

*(**HAYES** looks at **SANAM**.)*

What do you think?

SANAM. Me? It's the first time I'm hearing the speech.

HAYES. And what do you think? It's your paper too.

SANAM. It's good.

ARIEL. But...

SANAM. It's a little subjective, no? Sounds like a political speech?

ARIEL. Look, right after Philip gives this speech we're gonna do our PowerPoint with all the nitty gritty. It'll be super technical and objective and we'll cover all our bases but... I mean. This is political. We need people to understand what we're doing, to get excited about it. We need to save the bees, and we're like, ten, twenty, fifty years behind schedule.

HAYES. Ariel's right. It is political. It's personal. It's our future.

And you know who's going to be out there in that audience.

Chen, still stuck in that 2003 pollination experiment and milking it to glory. Middleton, who wouldn't understand a stochastic variation if he found it in bed with his mail-order wife. And let's not forget Roznovsky, the MacArthur idiot. Sixteen years of telling the world about a phantom bee disease and he still has the stones to show his face at our conference.

Ariel, you know, I say dial that up, I say let's give it to them.

ARIEL. You got it.

HAYES. Great, now let's see the presentation.

ARIEL. Uh, okay. So after you give the speech, you introduce us, we get up. And I start.

> *(She takes **SANAM**'s laptop, and taps a key to pull up the first slide.)*

"Good morning. It is an honor to be here, sharing our research on the effects of sub-lethal exposure to neonicotinoid pesticides, and its impact on the immunity levels and overall health of honey bee populations."

HAYES. I don't need all that, just show me the slides.

ARIEL. *(Not missing a beat.)* Moving on then. So we have –

> *(Tapping keys, skipping through the slides.)*

"Basic definitions, our field design, materials and methods, here's the literature review, here's the process I developed to test bee immunity levels, and here are my results over the course of six years of exposure to neonics."

What do you think of the pictures? Too gruesome?

> *(She looks at their reactions.)*

You did tell me to dial it up!

> *(Back to the presentation.)*

"And now, I pass it on to my esteemed colleague, research partner, and co-author, Sanam Shah, who will talk about her work in developing a pioneering quantitative model to measure population dynamics in honey bee colonies."

> *(She skips to the next slide, which we can tell, from their reactions, is either blank or obviously incomplete.)*

SANAM. Dr. Hayes, I'm not ready.

HAYES. Why not? Just put in the graphs.

SANAM. We have the old ones, yes, the ones we submitted with. But I'm having some issues with the new results.

HAYES. What issues?

SANAM. Something's going wrong, when I run the compilation.

> *(Beat.)*

When I input the new data, the 2016 data, the graph keeps skewing away from our projected results.

HAYES. Why?

SANAM. …I'm not sure.

HAYES. Must be a problem in the code.

SANAM. Probably. Hopefully.

HAYES. Hopefully?

SANAM. Hopefully it's just a problem in the code.

ARIEL. I mean, of course, it has to be. Sanam's been working really hard –

HAYES. – Why am I finding out about this now?

SANAM. Dr. Hayes, we only got the final batch of field data three weeks ago.

HAYES. You said you had enough time.

SANAM. I thought I did. This wasn't supposed to happen.

HAYES. *(To* **ARIEL.***)* Did something change? In the sampling methods? In the field?

ARIEL. No! We kept everything exactly the same.

HAYES. Then why is there a problem?

ARIEL. We'll find it, we'll fix it.

I told Sanam we could put in our existing projections for Monday, and –

HAYES. No. No, the NRDC wants to read our paper on Monday. We need the final results.

SANAM. But Dr. Hayes, what if I can't –

HAYES. Sanam, just...do your job.

(His phone beeps. His next meeting.)

I have to go. Meet me in my office tomorrow morning, show me what you have.

(He exits.)

(SANAM *sinks into her chair.)*

SANAM. What did he mean by that?

ARIEL. *(Pause.)* He means we need to debug the code. Let's get to work.

(SANAM *is quiet, lost. Gently – .)*

Hey.

(SANAM *sits up. She looks at her watch.)*

SANAM. Yes. Yes.

It's almost five o'clock. You should go.

ARIEL. I'll call the day care. I'll tell them I'm gonna be late.

SANAM. No, you should go pick up Rissi.

It's my problem. I'll fix it.

(ARIEL *starts gathering her things, putting on her jacket.)*

ARIEL. Don't kill yourself, okay? Don't stay too late.

SANAM. I can't. I have a date tonight, remember?

ARIEL. Oh god, that's tonight?

(Pause.)

I've told you this a million times before, but you don't have to go.

(SANAM *is already back at her computer.)*

SANAM. It's a free meal. You know I'll do anything for free food.

ARIEL. Need any help getting rid of him? I can burst in on the middle of your dinner, pretend you're my girlfriend, throw a drink in his face.

SANAM. It's fine. I'll do what I usually do.

ARIEL. *(Curious.)* What...*do* you usually do?

SANAM. I just be myself. They lose interest eventually.

(**ARIEL** *impulsively hugs* **SANAM** *from behind, and leaves.*)

(**SANAM** *types and watches the code compile.*)

Scene Three

(Later that night. At a fancy dinner place.)

*(**SANAM** sits with her blind date, **ARVIND**, who's in his mid-to-late thirties, not unhandsome.)*

ARVIND. *(Mid-story.)* And I wasn't gonna let the bastard slowroll me this time, I know how he plays. I got a pocket Jack and King heart right, and we got a ten heart in the flop, so that gets me excited about a flush. I mean, I'm no rube, it's like twenty-three to one at this stage, but you see those cards and you just gotta take your chances. So he checks, and I bet, but then he raises, and I'm like shit, what's going on. The turn's an Ace heart, and I'm like goddamn, I'm just one card away from a flush, one Queen away from a royal, and then he goes and raises again, like, taunting me, and now I gotta call bullshit or figure he might have two tens, which is like, what, a point four percent chance but still, if he got them, and the river card's a dud, I'm toast. So he's still makin' eyes at me, trying to get me to fold, but I knew what I was doing. I was tracking the cards, and I knew I was gonna get a heart, and I knew – I knew he was bluffing. So I went in, all the way in, just to give it to him, and the dealer flips over the river card, and fuck, wasn't just a heart, it was the Queen. Queen of Hearts, baby. Royal fucking flush. Three hundred K easy over. In my pocket. That's why I never hit the casinos in Vegas. The real action – the real money – happens underground. But then I bumped into Tom Brady in the men's room at the Bellagio, and we got so fucked up, we blew it all, it was epic.

*(**SANAM** stares.)*

SANAM. How did our grandfathers know each other again?

ARVIND. *(Mouth full.)* What?

SANAM. Our grandfathers?

ARVIND. They played golf right? Back in the old country?

SANAM. Yes, that's all I know too.

ARVIND. You gonna finish that?

(*He helps himself to the food on her plate.*)

Octopus Carpaccio. Best fucking seafood in the Bay.

(*Eating.*)

You're very quiet.

SANAM. Well, you talk a lot.

ARVIND. So what do you like to do for fun?

SANAM. Fun?

ARVIND. Yeah, fun, you know like – recreation, getting your rocks off.

SANAM. I don't really need to. I mean work is...I just work. I watch TV sometimes?

ARVIND. Stop, you're blowing my mind.

You really not gonna finish this?

SANAM. I'm not a seafood person.

And to be honest I'd already eaten before I got here.

ARVIND. Seriously?

SANAM. I got hungry.

ARVIND. (*Looking at his smartwatch.*) You were the one who wanted to get dinner, at like, eleven.

SANAM. I know, I know, I'm sorry. I'm just – this big problem came up at work, and I had to stay late, and I wound up eating an entire bag of beef jerky from Trader Joe's.

(*Pause.*)

It wasn't bad. It was like, kosher teriyaki flavored.

ARVIND. So that's what you like, huh?

SANAM. I mean...

ARVIND. All right. Next time? We're getting steak. My buddy told me about this new place in San Fran – the béarnaise makes you want to kill yourself. In a good way.

SANAM. Next time?

ARVIND. Ooh, what, you're playing hard to get now?

SANAM. I'm just a little surprised that you assumed there would be a next time.

ARVIND. I'll be here through the weekend. Can't get married without going on a few dates first, right?

SANAM. *(Seriously.)* Are you joking? I can't tell.

ARVIND. Well. Why are we here?

SANAM. I –

I don't know why you're here, but I'm here because – your grandfather played golf with my grandfather.

ARVIND. You play golf?

SANAM. No.

ARVIND. You have to try it. I usually do the rounds at Van Cortlandt in the Bronx. Maybe Tom and Giselle would like to join us next time they're in the city.

SANAM. Look. I – I don't know what my parents told you, but – I have no plans to go to New York any time soon. I still have to finish my thesis, and I'm hoping to stay on here as a post-doc.

>   *(**ARVIND** eats her octopus, smirking.)*

What?

ARVIND. I love watching people waste their potential. It's like a reality TV trainwreck but better.

SANAM. Waste my potential?

ARVIND. I mean, I've read your resume. You won the International Math Olympiad when you were in Delhi, didn't you?

SANAM. Yes, a while ago.

ARVIND. I bet Goldman Sachs, Deloitte, Morgan Stanley –

SANAM. Yes, they, they got in touch.

ARVIND. But you go on to do your masters in some podunk village university, and then when you decide to come to the states, you come to this podunk town – which, granted, has the best seafood in the Bay – to count bees and make what, thirty-two thousand a year?

(Pause.)

Shit, thirty-one?

(Pause.)

Shit, really?

SANAM. Are trying to win me over with this?

ARVIND. I don't need to win you over, that's the whole point of...this...arrangement.

SANAM. This is not a done deal.

ARVIND. I've looked at a lot of resumes.

SANAM. So have I.

ARVIND. *(Conclusive.)* And here we are.

We should get dessert. They make this bourbon lime cake here. Fucking insane.

SANAM. Look, unless you're planning on moving to this podunk town, as you call it, nothing's going to happen. There are no labs in the New York area that do the kind of research I do.

ARVIND. So? You can get another job.

SANAM. Why? I love my life here. I love my work.

ARVIND. Uh huh.

SANAM. My thesis – the project I've been working on for six years – it has pretty much solved Colony Collapse Disorder. I'm co-authoring a paper that's going to be published in *Nature*. Do you have any idea what a huge deal that is?

ARVIND. Colony Collapse Disorder.

SANAM. Yes. CCD.

ARVIND. You mean why the bees are disappearing, right? So like, hasn't that been solved a few times already?

SANAM. Well, there have been multiple theories. But the answer is simple. It's Monsanto pesticides.

ARVIND. Oh really.

SANAM. The chemicals they use – neonicotinoid compounds. They're obliterating the honey bee population.

ARVIND. It's kinda lazy, isn't it? Blaming everything in the world on Monsanto.

SANAM. Excuse me?

ARVIND. They're job creators. And innovators. How else are you gonna feed America?

SANAM. What do you know about Monsanto?

ARVIND. I trade their stocks.

SANAM. Of course you do.

> (**ARVIND** *looks at her.*)

ARVIND. I know a few analyst positions opening up in New York. Start with two fifty a year, maybe more, if you get in with the right people.

SANAM. I –

Wait, sorry, is this a job interview now?

ARVIND. Well it kind of is, isn't it?

> (*Pause.*)

So what do you say about that dessert? Or we can check out another place – I heard the drinks back at the Hilton aren't shabby.

> (*A moment.*)

SANAM. Something's bothering me.

> (*Pause.*)

If you don't mind my asking...how did you predict the river card – the Queen of Hearts?

ARVIND. What?

SANAM. In your – illegal poker game. Wait, even before that. How did you know your friend was bluffing? If one of his cards – just one – was a ten, which we can put at a ten percent likelihood, and the river card was a dud, which is like, an eighty percent chance, given the cards already on the table, then he wins. No question.

ARVIND. You play poker?

SANAM. No.

ARVIND. How the hell did you figure that out?

SANAM. Just tell me why you did it. The numbers don't add up.

ARVIND. You can't get caught up in the numbers too much. It's a game of imperfect information.

SANAM. If that's true...going all in was a terrible move. You were just lucky.

ARVIND. Lucky? You don't play the odds, you play people. That's why I kill at poker.

SANAM. *(Thinking.)* Did you...peek, or something?

ARVIND. What?

SANAM. He was raising so aggressively, there's no way you could have been sure he was bluffing unless you...

ARVIND. I don't peek. That's bush-league. How dare you.

SANAM. Sorry.

ARVIND. *(Pause.)* Someone else peeked.

SANAM. What?

ARVIND. The guy sitting next to him. Peeked. So all I had to do was check out his reaction. He smirked, and then folded. Which meant my buddy's cards were still good, but not great.

SANAM. But you still only had a twenty percent chance of getting a heart as the river card. It still doesn't make any sense, going all in.

ARVIND. Told you. I was tracking the cards.

SANAM. You can't "track" cards in poker, the sample size is much too small. You have five, and then what, six cards as your data set, out of fifty-two – you can't do anything with that.

ARVIND. But you're forgetting.

SANAM. What.

ARVIND. The sample size wasn't just that hand. It included every single round that came before it. This was the last game of the night. With the same dealer, same deck of cards. You could say there were...observable patterns.

SANAM. You're right. That's really smart of you.

ARVIND. Why, thanks.

SANAM. The results of every single round preceding would impact the statistical significance of the last round of... oh, wait. Wait.

ARVIND. What?

SANAM. What do you know about linear regression modeling?

ARVIND. What?

SANAM. Specifically Bayesian multivariate linear regressions. Analyzing stochastic variations across multiple levels of dependencies.

ARVIND. Like – probability models?

SANAM. Yes, exactly.

ARVIND. I know enough. I'm a quant guy. I use everything I can.

SANAM. If under twenty-five percent of the cards dealt were hearts in the earlier rounds, let's say the first three rounds, would you have made the same all-in bet?

ARVIND. What is this, a pop quiz?

SANAM. Just tell me.

ARVIND. I wouldn't. Not that early in the game. I wouldn't have had enough data by then.

SANAM. Right, because the results would not have been...

(Thinking furiously.)

Statistically significant. Shit.

ARVIND. I don't know what's going on here exactly but it's kinda turning me on.

SANAM. *(Not hearing him.)* Would you like to come back to my office and take a look at my calculations?

(A moment.)

ARVIND. Seriously? Right now?

SANAM. Yes now. It's –

(Looking at her watch.)

Past midnight. We'll have the whole place to ourselves.

ARVIND. Sure…if you're…if you're ready.

SANAM. Of course I'm ready. I just asked you. I have my lab keys right here.

> *(She jingles them.* **ARVIND** *immediately signals to the waiter for the bill.)*

Scene Four

(**SANAM** *and* **ARIEL**'s *office. Eerily quiet. The lights are dimly on.*)

(**SANAM** *waits for her program to start running, the light from the monitor illuminating her face.*)

(**ARVIND** *slowly looks around the room, taking it in. He takes off his jacket.*)

(*He picks up the stuffed honey bee.*)

ARVIND. Cute.

SANAM. Oh, Ariel should have taken that home. Rissi would like it.

ARVIND. Who?

SANAM. My research partner, Ariel. She has a kid.

ARVIND. Uh huh.

(**SANAM** *glances at her computer.*)

SANAM. The program takes some time to load.

(*Pause.*)

Do you know much about bees?

ARVIND. Nah, not really.

SANAM. They're really cool. Like, really, incredibly smart. Not individually, but collectively. The systematic way they forage for pollen is so data-driven and optimized that computer scientists have modeled an entire algorithm inspired by it.

ARVIND. Neat-o.

(*To* **SANAM**'s *relief, the coding program has loaded.*)

SANAM. Okay. So. This is where I am.

(*She steps back to let him see the computer screen and waits for his reaction.*)

ARVIND. ...Yeah, what am I looking at?

SANAM. Right. Uh...

(She thinks.)

Have a seat.

*(***ARVIND*** pulls up ***SANAM****'s chair and sits on it.)*

Our research is on Colony Collapse Disorder.

ARVIND. Yeah, you mentioned.

SANAM. *(Thinking hard as she talks.)* Figuring out why the bees are disappearing – it's possibly the ultimate mathematical challenge. Because even designing the experiment – there are so many variables to account for – not just the exposure level of pesticides, but other things we can't control, like, weather changes, and natural predators, and endemic diseases, and just random, year-to-year population fluctuations, which may or may not be significant.

*(***ARVIND*** leans back in his chair, playing with the stuffed honey bee, watching ***SANAM*** almost like she's performing for him.)*

Now Monsanto and other companies, for years, they've been pushing the narrative that pesticides alone can't be responsible for the bees dying. They say it's too complex to figure out, it's impossible to prove. Are you following me?

ARVIND. Yeah.

SANAM. Well, using Ariel's data from the field, I created a model that so rigorously controls for every possible variable – and variation within that variable – that we were able to isolate all other factors to prove that neonics – pesticides – are overwhelmingly responsible for the collapse of honey bee colonies.

ARVIND. Congratulations.

SANAM. *(Suddenly exploding.)* No! Don't congratulate me, because something's gone wrong!

ARVIND. Woah.

> (**SANAM** *tries to compose herself.*)

SANAM. A few months ago we submitted an early draft of our paper, that's the one that's going to be published in *Nature*. Next Monday, here in Santa Cruz, there's going to be the biggest ecological conference of the year, and my professor is being awarded with their top honor. All because of our research. But about a month ago, *Nature* asked us to include just one more batch of field data in the analysis.

ARVIND. Why?

SANAM. They want to make sure the paper is as robust as it can be. CCD studies are very competitive.

> (*She turns to her computer.*)

So anyway...when I do what they ask – when I input the most recent samples from the field, into my model – the results skew. Like they've never skewed before. Basically...the results are no longer significant.

ARVIND. So that means...

SANAM. If they're not significant, we have nothing.

> (**ARVIND** *gets up and comes closer to her, looking at the monitor.*)

ARVIND. Hmm.
Well.

> (*Pause.*)

Looks like the hippies lost.

SANAM. (*Horrified.*) This is not a joke!

ARVIND. Hey, relax. Okay. What do you want me to do?

SANAM. I need a simple fix. I think I might have made a mistake, somewhere, in the model, and I'm hoping it's a simple mistake. Something that I can fix, so that the results can go back to where they were.

ARVIND. And you're sure the data's clean.

SANAM. Yes, it's clean. And nothing's changed with the sampling methods, or the design.

(ARVIND steps away, considering. He turns back.)

ARVIND. So it used to be significant, but once you put in the new data, it's not.

SANAM. Yes.

(ARVIND shrugs.)

ARVIND. Just oversample the old data. They're not gonna notice.

SANAM. I can't do that.

ARVIND. Sure you can. Back when I worked in securities, we'd tweak the face value of mortgage-backed loans, just a tiny bit, and boom, suddenly we're sitting on a bundle worth twice the original valuation.

SANAM. Are you telling to use the same shady methods that created the Recession?

ARVIND. Hey, "created" is kind of a strong word.

SANAM. Just, help me, please. What could I have missed?

(ARVIND sits back down on the chair, thinking.)

ARVIND. Well, I don't really know much about ecology stuff, but uh...you took care of any replications?

SANAM. Yes, we controlled for that.

ARVIND. And you ran a sensitivity analysis at the beginning?

SANAM. Yes, done.

ARVIND. And I'm guessing you're using a non-parametric test.

SANAM. Yes.

ARVIND. It's tricky. The more complicated your model is, the harder it is to figure out whether it's telling you the truth.

SANAM. Yes, Arvind, everyone knows that!

ARVIND. I'm trying to help.

SANAM. Sorry.

(A pause.)

ARVIND. Let's take a step back. How long have you been doing this?

SANAM. The analysis? Six years. But Ariel had actually started the field work a year before that.

ARVIND. Six years, huh? So...if you've been getting significant results, all this time, until, just now...sounds like...well, sounds like the threshold effect.

> (**SANAM** *is quiet.* **ARVIND** *gets up and points at her dramatically.*)

Aha! You were biased.

SANAM. No.

ARVIND. There's always the possibility for data to, you know, swing the other way after it reaches a certain limit. But you didn't anticipate it. Because you work in a left-wing incubator of bad ideas, and you were biased.

SANAM. There's...no.

> (*He comes closer.*)

ARVIND. Damn, you seem so certain. Like you've already made up your mind. What's another word for that again?

SANAM. (*Annoyed.*) Shut up.

> (*A moment.*)

> (*He looks at her.*)

ARVIND. You seem a bit tense.

SANAM. I am tense.

ARVIND. (*Very close.*) I can help you with that.

SANAM. (*Confused.*) What?

ARVIND. You know you look really good, in this...fluorescent light.

> (*He moves in and* **SANAM** *panics.*)

SANAM. What? What are you doing?

> (**ARVIND** *steps away.*)

> (*A moment.*)

ARVIND. You asked me here...back to your office...to show me your calculations.

SANAM. *(Stammering.)* Yes, and I...showed you my calculations.

> *(A long moment.)*

ARVIND. Right. Okay.

> *(He reaches for his jacket.)*

SANAM. Wait.

> *(**ARVIND** is like...for what?)*

Please. Please stay.

ARVIND. Really?

SANAM. But only to talk.

ARVIND. That's enticing.

SANAM. I need... I need an outsider's perspective right now. I need to figure this out, I have to.

There could have been something I overlooked, in the initial equations, in the model itself.

ARVIND. It's possible.

SANAM. Just help me figure it out. Please. It'll be fun!

> *(**ARVIND** sighs and drops his jacket back on the couch.)*

ARVIND. What the hell.

Weirdest first date ever.

> *(**SANAM** tugs on his sleeve, almost shyly, and brings him to her computer. She scrolls up to the top of her coding program.)*

SANAM. Okay, so at the very top of the sequence, we're looking at the classic logistic equation for population modeling. That's dP over dT equals kP multiplied by one minus capital P over capital K –

ARVIND. Wait, hold on.

> *(He finds a marker in **SANAM**'s pen stand, and goes up to one of the lab windows, and starts writing down the equation on the glass.)*

DP over DT you said?

SANAM. What are you doing? Stop that.

ARVIND. Come on. I've always wanted to do this. Like in the movies.

SANAM. Arvind!

(She tries to grab the marker from him and he doesn't let her.)

ARVIND. I need this. I'm a visual thinker. You want me to help or not?

(A moment.)

SANAM. Fine. Okay. Fine.

(Reciting it from memory.)

That's DP over DT which equals k minus little P multiplied by one minus capital P over k, where K is the carrying capacity –

ARVIND. *(As he's writing this down.)* Still pretty hot to meet a girl who's good at math.

SANAM. You don't meet many girls, do you.

(They look at each other.)

ARVIND. Just tell me the equations.

SANAM. *(Continuing.)* So when we look at the analytic solution for that, it's P multiplied by t which equals K over one plus Ae...
You know it's faster if I just do it.

*(She grabs the marker from him and continues to write on the window. **ARVIND** looks at her, amused.)*

Scene Five

(The next morning in **HAYES**' *office.* **ARIEL** *and* **SANAM** *sit,* **SANAM** *in the same clothes she wore the previous day.* **HAYES** *at his desk.* **ARIEL** *looks at* **SANAM** *in concern.)*

ARIEL. Philip, would it be okay if we met later today? I think Sanam needs to get some sleep.

SANAM. I'm fine. The situation won't change if I go to sleep.

HAYES. All right. Sanam. Why don't you take us through this again. Just so we're clear what your issue is.

SANAM. When I run the compilation, the p-value comes up greater than alpha. It's .08 all of a sudden, when it should be .05, or less.

The results are not significant anymore.

ARIEL. I don't get it, they were significant a month ago. They were significant when we submitted and got accepted into *Nature*.

SANAM. Yes, they were.

ARIEL. So...

SANAM. When I input our final batch of field data, like they asked, it's tipping the scales, so to speak. No, that's a terrible analogy, this is nothing like scales, this is – this is –

*(***HAYES*** holds up a hand. ***SANAM*** stops.)*

HAYES. Look, we don't have to be a one hundred percent certain. We only have to be ninety-five percent certain. Are we ninety-five percent certain?

SANAM. I can't say – that's not – those kinds of confidence tests only work for simple, linear models. Our experiment is too complex.

(He sighs.)

HAYES. What do you need from me?

SANAM. I need more time.

HAYES. You have three days.

SANAM. No, I mean, I think we really need more time. We may have to extend the experiment.

ARIEL. What?

HAYES. What?

SANAM. When you think about it, in the overall scope of things, these are very preliminary results. Our paper will be so much stronger if we incorporate data from another round of sampling. Maybe two. Or three, why not.

HAYES. We can't extend the experiment.

SANAM. But do we – do we have to publish so soon?

ARIEL. What?

HAYES. This project is already two years behind schedule.

>   (**ARIEL** *throws up her hands.*)

ARIEL. I don't understand this at all. My last batch of field data tipped the scales?

SANAM. I shouldn't have said that. It didn't tip the scales – it – it – it broadened the scope. Look.

>   (*She grabs a marker and draws on a whiteboard.*)

This year, we have a slight deviation from our projected growth rate – the population exceeded our projected rates, which altered the significance level to .08 instead of .05. Our results are not significant.

ARIEL. That's it? That's what's fucking us over here? A .03 gap?

SANAM. It matters.

ARIEL. This makes no sense to me. Neonics are killing the bees. I know it, you know it, everyone knows it.

SANAM. This doesn't disprove it. It just means the results are not significant.

ARIEL. So can we publish or not?

>   (**SANAM** *shrugs, "no?"*)

How did *Nature* even accept our manuscript if we were on such shaky ground?

SANAM. We weren't. We're not. This is still – very promising. But to test out whether this is just a temporary blip in the data, or whether it's the truth – I believe we need at least three more years of fieldwork.

ARIEL. *(Snapping.)* We don't have three years!

*(A moment. **ARIEL** gathers herself.)*

Those morons at Stanford are just waiting, just nipping at our heels. They'll publish before us. And forget them. You know what, forget them. We *as a species,* do not have three years. Three years?! We lost forty percent of the American honey bee population from the beginning of this year alone. And sales of Monsanto products are *growing.*

SANAM. *(Quietly.)* I know.

ARIEL. How is this happening wow? After five years of incredibly positive results?

*(**SANAM** is about to reply – .)*

HAYES. *(Interrupting.)* It doesn't matter now, does it. Sanam. Tell me.

Why did we not anticipate this?

*(**SANAM** is quiet.)*

Right. You may go.

SANAM. Go...where?

HAYES. Go. Get to work.

SANAM. Doing...what?

HAYES. We have a conference on Monday. A submission deadline in four weeks. The biggest environmental advocacy group in the nation waiting on our results. We need to give them something, don't we?

SANAM. ...Yes?

HAYES. So get to work. You have the data, nearly seven years of it. You have your model. Now let's show them what neonics are actually – definitively – doing to the honey bees.

> (**SANAM** *gets up, confused, looks at* **ARIEL**, *and exits.* **ARIEL** *gets up to follow her.*)

Stay a minute.

> (**ARIEL** *sits back down.*)

> (*Pause.*)

You look tired.

ARIEL. Tired? I – I feel like I've been hit by a truck.

> (**HAYES** *sits down on his chair and leans back.*)

HAYES. PMS.

ARIEL. What?

HAYES. Publication Misery Syndrome. That's what we called it in my day

> (*Off her look.*)

It's a joke.

ARIEL. Philip, what are we going to do?

HAYES. (*Slowly, thinking.*) Are there any problems with your half of the paper?

ARIEL. No.

HAYES. Good. Good.

That's good to know.

> (*Pause.*)

Do you have anything lined up after graduation? A job, a fellowship.

ARIEL. Uh, no, not yet. It's been...you know.

HAYES. Spivak and a couple of her colleagues are flying out from D.C. to attend the conference.

ARIEL. Okay.

HAYES. I'm picking them up from the airport on Sunday night, and we're going to have dinner in my home. Would you like to join us?

ARIEL. Me?

Of course – of course I'd love to join you.

HAYES. I'm not making any promises, but think of it as a job interview.

They're very interested in you – in your background, your life story, your activism.

ARIEL. What do they know about me?

HAYES. Well, they've read your work – or the abstracts, at least. And they know that you're like me – first in your family to ever make it to college, hell, make it out of your home town. Succeeding on merit alone, no handouts, no legacy connections, no safety net. Plus, a single mom? Fighting the good fight? Of course they want you on their team.

If the congressional hearings happen, they're going to put you front and center, leading the charge. The media's going to love you.

ARIEL. But wait – wait – I don't understand. How is any of this going forward? How are we going to publish now? You heard what Sanam said.

HAYES. She's here to serve the project. As are you. As am I. It's the only thing that matters.

ARIEL. But if the results don't hold up –

HAYES. Mathematicians like to pretend there is some absolute truth out there. But mathematics doesn't give us a direct link to god, to the universe. It's man-made. A tool to help us make sense of our existence. To help us tell a story about who we are, and why things work the way they do. So the question is – what is the story we are going to tell?

(*Pause.*)

There is something Sanam's not telling us, and I can promise you, that's where the answer lies. If we look at the same numbers we have – the same data set – through a slightly different perspective, we'll get the results we need. Can you work with her?

ARIEL. I'm not a statistician.

HAYES. That might be an advantage here. That's why the two of you make such a good team. You complement each other. You help see things from another perspective. Help fill in the gaps.

(Pause.)

She needs to make sense of the results, for herself. Help her...get there.

(**ARIEL** *takes a second.*)

ARIEL. I'll try.

HAYES. Thank you.

ARIEL. *(Pause.)* How are you?

HAYES. I'm fine. But thank you for asking.

ARIEL. How's Alex?

HAYES. He's eight. He's...doing as well as can be expected.

ARIEL. I spent my whole childhood wishing my parents would split up. You did the right thing.

HAYES. And how old is young Artemis now?

ARIEL. Rissi? She just turned two.

HAYES. Already. So it's been almost two years since Sean, uh...hmm. Well. You're better off. Things end for a reason. At least, that's what I tell myself.

(A moment.)

ARIEL. I'll get to work then.

(**ARIEL** *gets up to leave. She pauses at the exit.*)

Thank you. For...taking a chance on me. More than once.

HAYES. That's what we do. We look out for each other.

(Pause.)

Don't let me down.

(**ARIEL** *nods and exits.*)

Scene Six

(Inside ARIEL's cozy apartment. ARIEL and SANAM sit on the floor, working. Maybe the stuffed honey bee from Scene One has made its way here.)

(They talk in low voices, there's a toddler sleeping in the other room.)

ARIEL. Where are we?

SANAM. Just about to run the regression analysis.

ARIEL. Do you still need the tables from batch two point six?

SANAM. Uh, no, actually, that's fine. I already went over that.

ARIEL. Okay. Well, this is my last notebook.

SANAM. This is our last analysis.

(Rissi starts crying. ARIEL goes into the bedroom.)

(SANAM's phone beeps on the coffee table. She looks at it, surprised at who the message is from.)

(A moment. Rissi is quiet again.)

(ARIEL comes back in.)

ARIEL. *(Quietly.)* Okay. She is officially *officially* asleep.

(Pause.)

For now.

(Pause.)

Listen. Hon. Even if – and I say this, as a big if – the results are not as spectacular as we thought they would be – we just need to give them something.

(Pause.)

So where are we with the regression analysis?

SANAM. Almost done.

> (**ARIEL** *sits down on the couch. She takes a deep breath. Then* **SANAM** *does.*)

ARIEL. Think it'll work?

SANAM. Probably not.

> (*Pause.*)

ARIEL. Is it done?

SANAM. Yes.

> (**SANAM** *turns around her computer and shows her.*)

ARIEL. And that is...

SANAM. Same thing. We're getting the same results.

> (*Putting her head in her hands.*)

We're fucked.

ARIEL. We're not fucked. Don't say that. There must be something we haven't tried yet.

SANAM. We've tried everything.

ARIEL. What about your professor over at Applied Math? What did she say?

SANAM. She said we're fucked.

ARIEL. You know what. You need a break. I'll make us some more tea.

SANAM. I don't want any more tea.

ARIEL. Want some food?

SANAM. No.

ARIEL. Let's go for a walk. I'll get the stroller.

SANAM. Are you mad? It's past midnight.

ARIEL. Shit, it's that late?

SANAM. Maybe I should just –

ARIEL. No, stay, we still have like – nine hours before we have to meet him.

SANAM. I'm exhausted.

ARIEL. How about I draw you a hot bath. Maybe that's how you'll find the answer. Hey, it worked for Archimedes.

(A moment.)

SANAM. What is this answer you want me to find? We have the answer. You do understand that, right? We have the answer. It's just not the answer we want.

ARIEL. *(Pause.)* I can't accept that.

SANAM. Why?

ARIEL. Why? Because it completely goes against my half of the paper. I watched honey bees die in the field for seven years. Hell, I've been watching them die for as long as I can remember. From when I was a kid.

My parents would take me with them, I would sit in the truck, our trailer packed with hundreds of crates, millions of bees. We would drive from farm to farm, our bees pollinating acres of almond trees and fruit groves. And guess when the trouble started. When these farms – that we'd been working with for years – when they started switching to neonics. One year, our hives were in peak condition, the next year, we're losing almost half of our colonies. Practically overnight. They just – vanished! And my parents weren't the only ones who lost their business, everywhere we looked, smaller beekeepers just couldn't keep up with the losses. And everyone had the same story. Everyone knew what was happening.

Look. Honey bees thrive, they flourish, they're practically indestructible until they come into contact with industrial, nicotinic pesticides. There is no other answer.

SANAM. *(Pause.)* It's anecdotal evidence.

ARIEL. It's not anecdotal –

SANAM. Technically it is. That's why we do this. That's why I'm here. That's why we need this model, we need the math. Because we're human. We see what we want to see.

(The air is getting tense.)

ARIEL. I didn't just imagine it, Sanam.

SANAM. No one is saying that you did.

> *(Rissi is crying again.)*

ARIEL. Oh, for fuck's sake.

SANAM. I'll go.

> *(**SANAM** goes into the bedroom.)*

> *(We hear **SANAM** soothe the baby.)*

> *(**SANAM***'s phone beeps again. **ARIEL** automatically glances at it.)*

> *(**SANAM** comes out.)*

ARIEL. *(Quiet, grateful.)* Thank you.

SANAM. You need a break too.

ARIEL. You're so good with her.

SANAM. *(Shrugging.)* I like kids.

ARIEL. *(Ruefully.)* I like bees.

> *(They smile at each other. **SANAM***'s phone beeps again. She looks at it and picks it up.)*

Who's texting you?

SANAM. The guy I met the other night.

ARIEL. Oh, right, how did that go? Was the free meal worth it?

SANAM. *(Pause.)* It was fine.

ARIEL. Yeah?

SANAM. Yeah, he was um – he was…actually, I had a really interesting talk with him about statistics.

ARIEL. Really?

SANAM. I mean. He thinks we're biased against Monsanto.

> *(**ARIEL** chuckles derisively.)*

ARIEL. What a douche.

SANAM. But…we…we are, though.

We are biased against Monsanto.

ARIEL. Am I biased against the willful destruction of our planet? Yeah, I think I'm allowed to have an opinion on that.

(Pause.)

You keep going quiet.

SANAM. He just made me...consider certain things. That's all.

ARIEL. Jesus, is that what's going on? You go on one date with some random Republican and he gets into your head at the last minute?

SANAM. I don't know if he's a Republican, I don't know why you're assuming that.

ARIEL. He thinks we're biased against Monsanto, huh? Did he say we're waging some kind of class war? Punishing job creators?

SANAM. ...How did you know?

ARIEL. Because I know these guys.

Biased against Monsanto. My ass.

Does bias explain how we were able to get five years of definitive, rigorous results? Has any other team in the world been able to do that? No. Not even close.

SANAM. That should have been a tip-off.

Why were we getting those results in the first place?

ARIEL. Because we're smarter and better than everyone else.

SANAM. We're competing at the top of our field. Everyone is as smart and as good as we are.

ARIEL. But no one cares as much as we do. Think of all those clowns in your field – all those idiot men – who keep getting published and hired and getting tenure while dismissing you and your work. But have any of them been able to develop the model that you have? Not a single fucking one of them. And I am the only CCD scientist who is actually from the beekeeping community, who knows and understands honey bees better than most human beings. Okay? That is why we've been getting these results.

SANAM. You just answered your own question. We care too much. We fell victim to confirmation bias.

ARIEL. What?

SANAM. When Philip asked me why I didn't anticipate this, I didn't tell him about the wrong decision that we made together.

(*Pause.*)

God, you really don't remember?

(*Pause.*)

Have you been thinking I made this huge colossal mistake all by myself?

ARIEL. If...that were case... I'm not blaming you.

SANAM. That's so generous of you, thanks.

ARIEL. Why are you getting angry? Just...talk to me.

(**SANAM** *takes a breath.*)

SANAM. With the passage of time and the accumulation of data, there is always the possibility for the initial results to lose their significance. It's called the threshold effect.

ARIEL. That applies here?

SANAM. It applies everywhere.

ARIEL. Then why we didn't anticipate it?

(**SANAM** *grabs one of* **ARIEL***'s notebooks – one that she's set aside by her laptop – and starts flipping through it.*)

SANAM. We did. Two years ago.

(*She lands on the page she was looking for.*)

It's right here. You wrote it down.

(**ARIEL** *takes the notebook and looks at it. She takes a second to read.*)

ARIEL. We were going to team with the Wilson farms to expand the size of our plots –

SANAM. We talked about expansion. The smaller the sample size, the less reliable the results, the more likely we'd get a false positive. So in order to be safe, we were going to expand.

ARIEL. So we – yes I remember – I do remember – we talked about this. But why didn't we expand when we...

SANAM. Look at the date on your notes.

ARIEL. ...Oh.

SANAM. Yeah.

(A long, awful pause as **ARIEL** *slowly realizes what happened.)*

ARIEL. I mean, we couldn't expand the fieldwork when I – literally couldn't be in the field in three weeks. I was going to have a baby. I was going on maternity leave.

SANAM. Yes, so we decided not to expand. We put undergrads in the field, and kept doing what we were doing.

ARIEL. But I guess that didn't...

(It finally sinks in.)

Fuck me.

(A long silence.)

Our experiment is flawed.

SANAM. Yes.

ARIEL. It's not a superficial error. It's not a mistake in the analysis. It's in the design.

SANAM. Yes.

ARIEL. Jesus Christ. Jesus *Christ* Sanam. What the everloving *fuck.*

(Rissi suddenly fusses again. They hold their breath, but she goes back to sleep.)

(Whispering.)

And it's my fault.

Oh god.

No.

I chose to have the baby and now...we're here.

SANAM. I knew the risks. But there was a part of me that didn't want to change anything, because the results we were getting were so amazing.

So...we made the call.

ARIEL. ...Why didn't you tell me?

SANAM. Tell you what?

ARIEL. Warn me...that...this could happen. If I stayed pregnant.

I've given up everything for this project, Sanam.

Everything.

I gave up – I chose this project over Sean. Over leaving with him, and his fancy new fellowship. Over giving Rissi an actual father. For all his faults he was going to help me raise her, and I chose to stay here and see this project through. Because we were only halfway done, and I knew we were on the verge of something amazing, and I couldn't abandon you, could I.

I chose to be a single mom for this fucking project, what the hell was I thinking?

(A pause.)

SANAM. You made the right decision.

ARIEL. How can you say that?

SANAM. In the larger scheme of things, you made the right decision.

ARIEL. In the larger scheme of things, honey bees are going to be extinct before the decade is over. And now, we can't do anything about it. Fuck EVERYTHING.

SANAM. Shh.

ARIEL. I've failed my child.

SANAM. What? No, you haven't. She's going to be fine.

Kids grow up in all sorts of families these days, they turn out fine.

ARIEL. She's going to live in a time of devastating food shortages. She's going to witness an ecological crisis we'll never be able to recover from.

SANAM. That's not for certain.

ARIEL. That's where we're going.

SANAM. Even if that's the case –

ARIEL. It IS. Why are you talking like that?!

SANAM. *(Pause.)* You're right. It's bad. It is.

I just...

I can't...

> *(Pause.)*

Ariel. Did you seriously think this one research paper would stop that from happening?

> (**ARIEL** *gathers her thoughts.*)

ARIEL. Maybe not this one paper. Maybe it won't change the world overnight.

Maybe they'll ignore it. They probably will.

But I cannot live with myself if we don't try.

> *(A moment.* **SANAM** *really has nothing to say.)*

> (**ARIEL** *goes to* **SANAM**'s *computer, looking at it.*)

> *(Pause.)*

I have a question.

SANAM. Yeah?

ARIEL. The last batch of data is the one screwing us over, right?

SANAM. Uh...yeah.

> *(A long moment.)*

ARIEL. Why can't we just move the samples around a little bit? In the model. Prioritize the old data.

> (**SANAM** *sits up.*)

SANAM. You mean oversample the old data?

ARIEL. Yeah.

SANAM. We can't.

ARIEL. Why not?

SANAM. Because that's not how the model works.

ARIEL. But would we get significant results? If we did it?

SANAM. That doesn't mean...

ARIEL. But would we?

SANAM. Yes, but that doesn't mean we can do that.

ARIEL. *(Getting worked up.)* Remember what the MIT guys did? With the varroa mites study last year? They were blaming CCD on mites. *Mites.* And didn't you say that was like – like blatant manipulation of data? Most of their funding was corporate, for god's sake. And they still got tons of press. And another year passed and nothing was done about Monsanto.

SANAM. So you're saying we should do what they did?

ARIEL. But in our case, we're *right.*

SANAM. That doesn't matter.

ARIEL. Look.

Statistics is how we make sense of our world, right?

SANAM. In a way.

ARIEL. Mathematics tells us the story of who we are, why things work the way they do. It's a narrative tool.

SANAM. I...suppose you could say that.

ARIEL. Every single statement you make is couched in a "maybe."

SANAM. Because nothing is definitive. Everything is calculated within a margin of error.

ARIEL. If nothing is definitive, why can't we err on the side of what we know to be true?

SANAM. Because it's fraud!

(A long moment.)

ARIEL. Who's going to know?

SANAM. What?

ARIEL. *(Slowly.)* Who's going to know? Our paper's been through three rounds of peer review already. They're not gonna do another one. They're not gonna manually cross-check every single data point from our previous draft.

SANAM. That's beside the question.

ARIEL. And even if some questions were raised after – even if – do you think they'd be likely to print a retraction? On such an important issue?

SANAM. What if they do?

ARIEL. Nobody reads that shit! Nobody reads the retractions.

SANAM. I do. I read all of them!

ARIEL. Oh god.

SANAM. I don't think you understand what you're asking of me. You're asking me to put out a fabricated paper.

ARIEL. It's not like we're making up something from scratch. We have five years of results. We're just smoothing the rough edges.

SANAM. *(Incredulous.)* Rough edges? What? What are you even talking about?

> *(Pause.)*

ARIEL. I know that it doesn't really matter to you what happens after graduation, but I need this. I need to publish to get a job, to get anything done.

SANAM. You think it doesn't matter to me?
I need a job as much as you do. I need to stay in this country.

ARIEL. But you'll be fine either way. Your parents will take care of you, but I don't have that. I have a kid that I'm responsible for.

SANAM. I have never asked my parents for anything. Ever since I left, I haven't –

ARIEL. But you can, and that's the point, you can. That's not how it is for most of us. Most of us don't have the luxury of-of-of even considering...
Look this project really matters to me. I've worked too hard on this to just let it go over a technicality.

SANAM. It's not a technicality! It's how the model works. It's trying to tell us something. The model is giving us a clue. The model that I built, that I worked so hard on all these years. The best thing I've ever done – the most advanced technique anyone has developed. It's beautiful.

And it's giving you an answer that you don't like. So you're pretending something's wrong with my research instead of – instead of – even considering the possibility that you might have been wrong.

ARIEL. *(Stunned.)* You think our hypothesis is wrong?

SANAM. Maybe.

ARIEL. So what do you think it is? What do you think? Mites? Diseases? Bad beekeeping practices? "Cell phone towers"? What is it? Which one of their talking points do you believe is the truth, instead of the obvious answer? Huh?

SANAM.	ARIEL.
I don't know.	"I don't know."
	Right?

(A moment.)

SANAM. The model indicates that it's not just the neonics.

ARIEL. Your model is wrong.

*(A beat. **SANAM** is trying hard not to lose it.)*

SANAM. Say that again? I just want to make sure I heard you right.

ARIEL. *(Clearly.)* Your model is wrong.

SANAM. Okay. The model is wrong? Okay.

Come here. Look at this.

*(She thrusts her laptop into **ARIEL**'s hands.)*

There. Take a look. Go on.

Show me where it's wrong.

Are you going to show me where the numbers are wrong?

I mean, I'm just getting my Ph.D. in this, but I guess you know better. Right?

Go ahead and fix it. I'm sure you've spent your whole life working to be the best at what you do. I'm sure you're one of a handful of people in the world who even understands what you're looking at.

Go on.

ARIEL. *(Shoving the laptop back at* **SANAM**.*)* Nice, Sanam. Real fucking nice. You know that's not what I'm talking about.

SANAM. Then what are you talking about?

ARIEL. I'm talking about you living in your head. Relying on these abstract arbitrary fucking concepts to decide what reality is, when the truth is staring us in the face. None of what you're obsessed with is real. None of it is real. My life is real. The bees dying, that's real. I mean if you don't care about what we're doing here, then why are you even doing this?

SANAM. Because I'm a *scientist.*

(A long pause.)

ARIEL. That's what you think of me, right? Not a real scientist. Just some hick from the Central Valley who faked her way into grad school.

SANAM. Well, stop acting like one.

*(**SANAM** gathers her laptop, her bag, and leaves without another word.)*

Scene Seven

(**ARVIND**'s *hotel room.* **SANAM** *stands at the door, looking a bit lost.* **ARVIND** *holds a drink, looking surprised but okay with this turn of events.*)

ARVIND. Hey.

SANAM. Hello.

ARVIND. Hi.

SANAM.	**ARVIND.**
Can I –	To what do I –
I was just –	So what made you –

SANAM. Can we be friends?

ARVIND. *(Pause.)* With benefits?

(**SANAM** *turns to leave.*)

Hey, hey. Wait. I'm kidding. It's a joke.

Wanna come inside?

SANAM. Sure.

(**SANAM** *comes in, looks around, still unsure of herself.* **ARVIND** *closes the door and heads to the mini-bar.*)

ARVIND. Can I get you a drink?

SANAM. Those things are expensive.

ARVIND. I'm not paying for it.

SANAM. I'll have a water.

ARVIND. A water, and...

(*He holds up two small liquor bottles.* **SANAM** *points.*)

SANAM. That one?

ARVIND. Good choice. Neat? On the rocks?

SANAM. With ice?

(**ARVIND** *grins and makes her a drink.*)

I don't really know why I'm here.

ARVIND. Well, it's nice to see you.

(He hands her the drink.)

You weren't exactly replying to my texts.

SANAM. It's been...a stressful time.

ARVIND. No kidding.

(He holds up his drink.)

To working till it kills us.

(They clink glasses. SANAM slowly sips her drink. ARVIND sits on the bed.)

You know it was pretty fun, the other night. Helping you out.

SANAM. Yeah, that was actually...quite helpful.

(SANAM is still standing, rod straight.)

ARVIND. Make yourself comfortable.

SANAM. Okay.

(She continues standing. He gets up and gives her the bed.)

ARVIND. Here.

(He sits in an armchair. SANAM sits on the edge of the bed.)

So how's it going?

(SANAM shrugs.)

Did you figure it out? Your problem?

SANAM. Uh...well. Figured out the source of the problem.

(Pause.)

You were right.

ARVIND. I was? Wait, what did I say?

SANAM. The threshold effect.

ARVIND. Oh yeah. Oh, man. That's too bad.

SANAM. Mm.

ARVIND. Confirmation bias, right? She's a bitch.

SANAM. *(Suddenly.)* Fuck!

ARVIND. Woah.

Potty mouth.

You okay?

SANAM. Everything is awful.

ARVIND. *(Grinning.)* Cheers.

> *(He clinks his glass with hers, and drinks.* **SANAM** *looks at him.)*

SANAM. So do you just not care about anything? Is that how you live your life?

ARVIND. Hey, I care about shit.

I care deeply about the Giants. Single-malt scotch. Gillian Anderson.

SANAM. *(Nonplussed.)* Yeah, I really don't know why I'm here.

ARVIND. That's what girls say when they don't wanna seem too forward, you know what I mean? But I like my ladies aggressive. I like them showing up at my hotel room at two in the morning, wearing...whatever that is.

SANAM. Okay. That's not why I'm here. Let's make that clear.

Absolutely not.

> *(**ARVIND** grins.)*

> *(**SANAM** sips her drink.)*

ARVIND. So what's up?

> *(**SANAM** doesn't say anything.)*

...Seriously, you okay?

SANAM. I just had an awful, awful fight with Ariel.

> *(Pause.)*

ARVIND. Mm-hmm.

SANAM. We've never fought before. We've never, ever raised our voices at each other, I can't even remember a time when we...

I said something terrible tonight.

ARVIND. What did you say?

SANAM. That I'm a real scientist, and she isn't.

ARVIND. ...That's it? That's the terrible thing?

SANAM. Well what if somebody called you not a real...

(*Confused.*)

I'm sorry, what is it you do again?

ARVIND. (*Amused.*) I'm a derivatives trader. But what does that matter?

SANAM. It matters, right? It's who you are.

ARVIND. Okay, wait. Let's back up. What – what happened?

SANAM. Well, our paper is dead. I've known that, since that night we figured it out. But Ariel wants us to publish anyway.

ARVIND. How?

SANAM. By...adjusting the model.

ARVIND. How?

SANAM. Oversampling the old data.

ARVIND. Hey, that was like the first thing I suggested.

SANAM. Yeah. And it's still a terrible idea.

ARVIND. Why?

SANAM. Why? Because it's unethical!

ARVIND. So why did she suggest it too?

SANAM. (*Pause.*) It means a lot to her. Getting the results we hoped for. She has all these big plans for the paper. Lobbying the big corporations. Passing legislation. Saving the world.

ARVIND. Everyone wants a bogeyman, right? An easy target. Take them down, and you feel a little better about yourself. But we're all terrible. At the end of the day, we're all terrible. And we're screwing everything up together. So why punish the guys who actually figured out how to make a little money along the way?

SANAM. (*Pause.*) Because she's a mom. She's a mom, and she has to save the world.

(*He considers her.*)

ARVIND. Would you guys get in trouble or something, if you did it?

SANAM. ...To be honest, probably not. People get away with this all the time.

ARVIND. Then why not?

SANAM. This is not how we're supposed to do it!

Research is so complicated, the only thing stopping fraud is ourselves.

This country already doesn't trust basic science, why give them more ammunition?

ARVIND. The people who don't trust science, just don't trust science. You can't do anything about that.

SANAM. That's so depressing.

ARVIND. *(Pause.)* And look, at the end of the day, it's not gonna make a difference. You know that, right? One academic paper versus a multi-billion dollar global industry? Come on.

SANAM. So...

ARVIND. If it's just gonna be a shout into the void, then why not just publish? It clearly means a lot to your friend.

SANAM. Because it's my work! I can't compromise on my work!

ARVIND. Why not?

SANAM. Because it's who I am!

It's all that I do.

Who am I without my work?

> *(Pause.)*

ARVIND. ...Well, that's pretty sad.

SANAM. What?

ARVIND. You think that's all you are? Just your work?

I mean...is that how you see *me*?

> *(Pause.)*

I'm more than what I do for a living.

You're a lot more than just your work.

(Pause.)

Look, life's messy. Compromise is part of the deal.

You wanna get anywhere? Do anything? Gotta compromise.

The question is what matters to you.

Like...yeah. You can stick to your principles and abort the paper, the question is whether that matters more to you than your relationship with your friend.

*(**SANAM** stares at him in surprise.)*

Anyway. It's your call, obviously.

I just thought it was a pretty weird way to make a decision.

(A moment.)

SANAM. We're not gonna save the world.

ARVIND. The world's gonna be fine.

SANAM. You're right. We're the ones who are fucked.

ARVIND. Do you want kids?

*(**SANAM** takes a moment to think about it.)*

SANAM. You know, despite my better judgement... I do.

ARVIND. Me too.

(A beat.)

SANAM. Why did you want to meet me? Why did you...ask to be set up?

*(**ARVIND** raises his glass.)*

ARVIND. Compromise!

SANAM. That's romantic.

ARVIND. Look, I'm officially in my late thirties. I'd been fucking around for a long time, and I had to figure out what actually mattered to me. And, so I did. It's... settling down...getting married...to someone really fucking cool.

SANAM. You think I'm really fucking cool?

ARVIND. Yeah.

(A moment.)

SANAM. This job.

(Pause.)

So much pressure.

(**ARVIND** *gets up to get another drink.*)

ARVIND. You don't have to tell me about pressure. Look at my face. I aged ten years, my first six months on Wall Street.

SANAM. It's a nice face.

(**ARVIND** *turns back in surprise.*)

ARVIND. What?

(They look at each other.)

(**SANAM** *puts her drink down, goes up to him, and kisses him.*)

*(For once, **ARVIND** is speechless. **SANAM** looks a bit confused as well.)*

(She kisses him again, and he responds passionately.)

SANAM. Don't tell your mother we're doing this.

ARVIND. Could we not...bring up our mothers right now?

SANAM. Good idea.

(They continue making out and fall back on to the bed.)

Scene Eight

(In **HAYES'** *office, the day after.* **HAYES** *isn't there yet.* **SANAM** *and* **ARIEL** *wait.* **SANAM** *sits.* **ARIEL** *looks out the window, squeezing the stuffed honey bee like a stress ball.)*

(They aren't talking.)

(Silence for a long, long time. **SANAM** *looks like she wants to say something, but doesn't know where to start.)*

*(***ARIEL***'s phone beeps. She looks at it.)*

ARIEL. He's on his way.

(Silence again, but of a different kind.)

(They hear footsteps.)

*(***HAYES** *enters.)*

HAYES. Good morning.

*(***HAYES** *takes off his coat and bag.)*

Who died? Aside from all the honey bees.

(Pause.)

All right. Let's get to it. What do you have for me?

*(***ARIEL** *is turned away.* **SANAM** *doesn't quite know what to say.)*

Where's the new presentation?

SANAM. ...It's not ready yet.

HAYES. Why not?

(Pause.)

You realize the speech is tomorrow.

(Pause.)

What? What is the problem here?

*(***ARIEL** *looks at* **SANAM,** *finally. Resigned. She indicates, "go head, just say it.")*

SANAM. I just haven't had a chance to work on it yet. We were up very late last night.

HAYES. So where are we?

SANAM. We're fine.

ARIEL. What?

SANAM. We're fine.

Look, Dr. Hayes.

> *(She takes a piece of paper from his desk and starts sketching.)*

If we recalculate the earliest variants, we can position the final results within the realm of significance. The graph works. We're fine.

HAYES. *(Looking at the graph.)* Well, good. Good. Great work, both of you.

> *(Pause.)*

I'll be in today. Just get back to me when the presentation is ready.

> *(**SANAM** gets up, ready to leave. **ARIEL** looks at the graph on **PHILIP**'s desk.)*

ARIEL. Wait.

> *(**SANAM** pauses.)*

SANAM. What?

ARIEL. What are you...doing?

SANAM. I fixed the problem.

ARIEL. Did you really fix the problem?

> *(Pause.)*

Tell me if you really fixed the problem.

HAYES. It's fixed. She just said it.

ARIEL. Aren't you –

Don't you want to know how she fixed it?

HAYES. *(Pause.)* Do I want to know?

ARIEL. *(To **SANAM**.)* Did you oversample the old data?

> *(A beat.)*

SANAM. It's close enough, right? I mean, for almost six years this was what the model was telling us. So...

ARIEL. So you're...

SANAM. Smoothing the rough edges.

ARIEL. You're fine with this? Are you really?

SANAM. I thought this was what you wanted.

ARIEL. So you just –

Wow. You're making it worse. Do you know that?

I didn't think it was possible but you're actually making it worse.

SANAM. What are you talking about?

HAYES. Whatever's going on, you can figure it out between yourselves. Come back with the presentation.

ARIEL. Didn't you – hear? She oversampled the old data to drown out the new batch. That's all she did. She's changing the rules to help us win.

HAYES. Sanam's the mathematician here and I think we should trust her expert judgement.

ARIEL. She doesn't know what she's doing.

SANAM. What? This was what you wanted – I'm doing what you wanted.

ARIEL. So you're willing to let go of everything just to – what – placate me? Just give in so I'd stop being mad at you, is that what you're doing here?

SANAM. I – what? How am I still the bad guy here?

ARIEL. Because you said what you said and you left – and you clearly think that I'm still – that I'm not really –

SANAM. Look, you had a point, okay? Even if neonics are not the entire answer, what's wrong with using this to go after Monsanto? Nothing. We should be doing it anyway.

ARIEL. So neonics are not the answer.

SANAM. Does it matter?

ARIEL. Yes it does!

It matters!

SANAM. I am very confused right now.

ARIEL. If we push this out, and neonics are not the real answer, then how will we ever actually find out what's going on? How will we ever actually stop CCD?

HAYES. That's not our job.

*(The **WOMEN** turn to him, surprised.)*

ARIEL. What?

HAYES. That's not our job. Figuring out what's really going on? There's no way. What kind of pie-in-the-sky thinking is that? Our job is to publish what we know.

ARIEL. But – we can't publish.

Her model is telling us that the results are not significant, so we can't publish. We can't do the presentation tomorrow.

HAYES. That would be my decision now, wouldn't it?

(A moment.)

*(**HAYES** holds up **SANAM**'s hand drawn graph.)*

How obvious is this?

SANAM. What?

HAYES. How...obvious are the changes?

*(**SANAM** looks at **ARIEL**, conflicted.)*

SANAM. It would be almost impossible to tell. To prove it you'd need the original indexes of our source data –

HAYES. – which won't be in the paper, of course.

(Pause.)

All right.

(Pause.)

We're publishing. Moving forward as planned.

(Pause.)

You can go now.

*(**HAYES** back gets to work at his desk.)*

SANAM. *(Tightly.)* Thank you, Dr. Hayes.

(**SANAM** *moves to leave, when* **ARIEL** *speaks.*)

ARIEL. Philip...

(*A long pause.*)

HAYES. Do you have something to say?

(*A pause.*)

Our paper is fine. The truth hasn't changed.

(*Pause, starting to get angry.*)

Do I have to spell everything out for you?

(*A moment. The* **WOMEN** *look at each other.*)

This is my call. My lab. My funding. My research. You have some qualms about it? Fine. I'm here to absolve you.

ARIEL. So...you're going take the fall, if this ever gets out?

HAYES. If *what* ever gets out?

Explain what you just said.

ARIEL. If – when – a statistician reads it, and suspects what we're doing –

HAYES. We welcome critiques. Won't change the fact that this will be a cover story in the world's most high impact science journal.

ARIEL. So that makes it all okay?

HAYES. I did not think you of all people would be this fucking naive.

ARIEL. And I didn't think you'd publish if we told you what was really going on!

HAYES. Of course I knew what was going on! I was giving you both time to work on the paper, get yourselves comfortable with the results.

SANAM. Comfortable?

HAYES. And you couldn't even pick up on that! Give yourselves a little wiggle room, some space to accept the experiment as it is. Who the fuck cares about a .03 gap in the likelihood of pesticides destroying human civilization? Seriously. A .03 gap from the anticipated results and we let the murderers walk, right?

Twenty years of bullshit research out there. People – charlatans – corporate rats – getting awards, funding, accolades, for deliberately looking away from the truth. For being complicit in the destruction of our planet. And now *I* have to hold myself to a higher ethical standard?

> (**ARIEL** *looks at* **HAYES** *like she's seeing him for the first time.*)

SANAM. So you – you knew all along that there was no real solution? You were just playing dumb? Waiting for me to...fudge the numbers out of desperation? Take it all on myself? *(To* **ARIEL.***)* Is that what you were doing?

ARIEL. No. I wasn't.

HAYES. I expected you to do your job, and you have. You've done your job, Sanam. You've saved the paper.

SANAM. No, I can't. No. This is...

(To both of them.) You have no respect for my work.

HAYES. This is not about your ego.

ARIEL. But this is her work. And it's mine. It's our paper. Look, why can't we just rewrite the conclusion – admit that we're not done yet.

HAYES. Null results do not get published. They don't get cited, they don't count.

ARIEL. Our project is still substantial. It's still important work.

HAYES. Important work? Right. I get up there tomorrow, I accept that fucking award, and say that after ten years of fieldwork, of groveling for every scrap of funding, we still have shit to show for it. That's what you expect me to get up and say, right?

ARIEL. Not in those exact words.

We can't... I can't lie for you.

HAYES. Fine. Have it your way.

ARIEL. What?

HAYES. If you don't have anything useful to contribute, you can remove your names from the paper.

ARIEL.   **SANAM.**

   WHAT?   No, that's not what we –

HAYES. It's up to you. If you want to contribute, stay. If not, no one is forcing you to be a part of this.

SANAM. This is seven years of our work!

ARIEL. You think you're going to publish a highly complex longitudinal study with no co-authors? Seriously?

HAYES. If I have to, yes.

ARIEL. No one will buy it.

HAYES. You're either in or you're out. Make your choice.

               (**ARIEL** *looks at* **SANAM**.)

ARIEL. I can't do this. If you publish, knowing that we've compromised the integrity of our research, I'm going to the review board.

HAYES. Well, that's a fucking joke.

ARIEL. Of both the university and the journal. People won't look too kindly on a graduate student's work being stolen from her.

HAYES. You're threatening me, Ariel? Threatening me, this lab, your own future?

ARIEL. I'm doing what you did. In your own career. Standing up against conventional thinking. Pushing forward to get to the truth.

HAYES. Let me make one thing clear. You would not be here, in this program, if I didn't decide to give you a chance against my better judgement. You would not be in this room right now, if I didn't do you the kindness of keeping you on this project – on *my project* – after you got knocked up. And now you think you can tell me what I can and can't do with my own research? What do you think is going to happen if you go to the review board? Think they'll listen to a community college charity case like you?

SANAM. *(Quietly.)* I'll do the same.

HAYES. What?

SANAM. I'll go to the review board.

HAYES. You can't be serious.

(Incredulous.) You...you can't be serious. No one does this. There is such a thing called loyalty.

ARIEL. And it goes both ways.

(**ARIEL** *gets up to leave.*)

HAYES. Where do you think you're going?

ARIEL. Go ahead and take my name off the paper. I'll be happy to answer any questions when they ask me why.

HAYES. You do this, and you are done. We are – done. Do you understand? You will get nothing from me going forward. No reference, no prospects, no hope.

ARIEL. I don't want anything from you.

(**ARIEL** *exits.* **HAYES** *stares after her in disbelief.* **SANAM** *is still there, startled, not sure what to do. A moment.* **HAYES** *looks at her.*)

HAYES. *(Say something or get out.)* What?

(**SANAM** *shakes her head, and exits.*)

(**HAYES** *sinks into his chair.*)

Scene Nine

(The next day. At the conference. SANAM is by herself. She watches people walk past. We can see that's she trying to get the nerve to just get up and go have a conversation with someone, but she can't. She fiddles with her conference badge. She looks miserable.)

(We hear announcements being made of talks about to start, seminars being rescheduled, usual conference business.)

(SANAM takes out her phone and checks her e-mail. She's received something interesting. She reads, looking confused.)

SANAM. *(Murmuring.)* What...

(She plugs in her earphones, and makes a call, disturbed.)

(Lights up on ARVIND in New York. Wearing a bluetooth device. Taking pictures of objects we can't see. He taps his headset and answers the call.)

ARVIND. Hey.

SANAM. What is this?

ARVIND. What?

SANAM. What did you e-mail me?

ARVIND. Oh, yeah, the article. Cool, right?

SANAM. What is this – honey bee colonies in the U.S. are at a twenty year high?

ARVIND. Good news, right? Your problem is solved. Now you can just move to New York already.

SANAM. *(Still reading the piece.)* It's a specious, misleading headline – must be some sort of paid media.

ARVIND. No, it's one of your liberal rags, the Washington Post.

SANAM. Still.

> *(She continues reading it on the phone, perturbed.)*

ARVIND. Monsanto solved your problem for you. Just like I always say. The free market figures it out.

SANAM. *(Getting worked up.)* Monsanto has applied a bandaid on the problem. They are artificially inflating honey bee population numbers through forced breeding. They are isolating and selling queen bees for fifteen dollars each – on Amazon.com? I mean...this is interesting, but this isn't the – this isn't the actual answer to the question. The question remains –

ARVIND. Hey.

SANAM. Yes?

ARVIND. *(Playful.)* Nothing.

> *(Pause.)*

Where are you?

SANAM. I'm at the conference.

ARVIND. Why the hell are you there?

SANAM. I don't know. I like to torture myself.

ARVIND. You wanna know where I am?

> *(He's sending a picture he just took.)*

SANAM. Sure, where are you.

> *(Her phone beeps.)*

ARVIND. Check your messages.

> *(**SANAM** stays on the line, checks her messages. Her jaw doesn't drop, exactly, but she's very surprised.)*

SANAM. Uh...okay.

ARVIND. Do you like it?

SANAM. I... I mean...

ARVIND. I'm right here in Harry Winston's – I mean there's a shit-ton of jewelry, I can find something you like.

(He takes more photos and texts them to her.)

There's this one. And this one. And this one. They call it a princess cut. I don't really know why.

(SANAM's phone beeps multiple times.)

SANAM. Arvind –

ARVIND. And this one –

SANAM. Arvind. I don't want a ring.

ARVIND. Why? Who doesn't want a ring?

SANAM. You know. Blood diamonds and all that.

ARVIND. You serious?

SANAM. Ariel calls it "capitalist murder glass." She'd kill me if she saw me wearing a diamond. If she didn't want to kill me already.

ARVIND. Okay. So what do you want?

SANAM. I don't know.

ARVIND. Look, I – I get it – I've been – I've been kind of flippant. About this whole thing. And maybe – maybe you deserve something super romantic, but I – I'm not there right now, and I just couldn't wait.
Sanam Shah. Will you marry me.

(A long pause.)

There's a tiara here that would look awesome on you.

(A moment.)

Well?

SANAM. This is moving a bit fast, isn't it?

ARVIND. You really think so?

SANAM. Yeah.

ARVIND. Look, I know what I want. And you – you know what you want too. That's what I like about you. So… why wait?
What do you say?

SANAM. Would you move here?

ARVIND. What?

SANAM. Would you move to Santa Cruz? Or – let's say wherever I get a job. Wherever I can continue my research. I don't know where I'll wind up.

ARVIND. If we get married, you don't have to work, you know that right?

SANAM. What?

ARVIND. I mean – work, like, work for money. I think you should do whatever you want. You could make a killing as an analyst, but if you don't want to do that, you don't have to be – you know – beholden to whatever university's gonna give you a job. You can live in New York, and do like, whatever the hell you want.

SANAM. But I am doing what I want.

ARVIND. Yeah, but here I'll support you. Financially. That's what I'm saying. So you have – you have more options, than just…this.

SANAM. So you won't move.

ARVIND. *(Really surprised.)* No.
My work is here.

SANAM. And it's more important than mine?

ARVIND. In purely objective terms? Yeah. I mean, yeah.

> *(A beat.)*

SANAM. I can't.

> *(A beat.)*

ARVIND. I just…
I think you're smart.

SANAM. Mm-hmm?

ARVIND. I think you could do better.

SANAM. Hmm.

> *(She doesn't say anything further.)*
>
> *(A beat.)*
>
> (**ARVIND** *exhales.*)
>
> (**SANAM** *blinks, feeling very sad.*)

ARVIND. So…

>*(Pause.)*

I should, um –

SANAM. We don't have to / talk about this right now.

ARVIND. / I should let you get back to your conference.

SANAM. *(Pause.)* Yeah. Okay.

>*(Pause.)*

Thank you for –

ARVIND. Take care, okay?

>*(A beat.)*

>*(He hangs up.)*

>*(**SANAM** stares at her phone.)*

>*(She dials.)*

>*(We hear ringing. Several rings. Then, we hear **ARIEL**'s voice – .)*

ARIEL. *(Voicemail.)* Hi there. You've reached Ariel Spiegel, I can't come to the phone right now, but –

>*(**SANAM** hangs up, frustrated, sad.)*

>*(She looks around. She should get up and go about her day. But she can't.)*

Scene Ten

(**ARIEL**'s *backyard. One day later. Sunset.*)

(**ARIEL** *wears protective beekeeping clothes and carries a smoker (to prevent bee stings) as she works on one of her personal bee hives. The hive is a multi-leveled wooden crate – a man-made hive favored by professional beekeepers.*)

(**SANAM** *slowly enters through the garden gate.*)

SANAM. Hi.

(**ARIEL** *looks up.*)

ARIEL. Hi.

(*A long pause.*)

SANAM. So, the conference is over.

ARIEL. Yeah?

(*She turns back to her hive.*)

How did it go.

SANAM. Not great.

Philip received the award, and then he got up, and gave like, the saddest speech in the world. Just said thanks, spoke vaguely about advancing the cause of ecology, then sat down with no news, no big announcement. The speech was so...short. People were talking about how weird it was.

And then he spotted me in the audience. I don't think he expected me to show up. He looked...

Ariel, no one's ever hated me before.

ARIEL. He doesn't hate you. He hates me.

SANAM. (*Pause.*) Do you hate me?

(**ARIEL** *shakes her head, tired, not wanting to engage.*)

ARIEL. Why did you come over?

SANAM. Can I not see you anymore?

ARIEL. I'm just a little busy right now.

SANAM. Ariel, please.

ARIEL. What?

SANAM. *(Voice quivering.)* Just, please, I feel like I'm going mad.

>   *(Pause.)*

I just want to talk to you.

ARIEL. What do you want to talk about.

SANAM. Stop it.

>   *(Pause.)*

I'm so sorry, Ariel, I really am.

ARIEL. I know.

SANAM. Stop punishing me.

ARIEL. I'm not punishing you. What are you talking about?

SANAM. You didn't pick up my calls.

ARIEL. I've barely been able to get out of bed, much less answer the phone.

SANAM. I've been miserable. I don't care about the paper, about jobs, about anything. I've never been so miserable my entire life. I don't know what I would do without you.

>   *(A moment.)*

ARIEL. I just need some time.

SANAM. Okay.

>   *(A moment.)*

ARIEL. I don't hate you.
I'm...angry.

SANAM. At me?

ARIEL. A little. At the situation, really. At myself. Mostly.
I feel so...useless.

*(A long moment. **SANAM** stands where she is, hugging herself against the evening chill. **ARIEL** continues working on her hive.)*

I was thinking. You know...all we can hope for is that we leave our world a little bit better than when we found it. Like, that's the meaning of life, as far as I'm concerned. And I don't know if we're doing that. I honestly don't know if we can. But these...these amazing little things. Every single honey bee does that. It's built into their design. By default, they leave the world better than when they came into it. It's that simple.

*(**SANAM** is still, listening.)*

Are you cold?

SANAM. I'm fine.

ARIEL. Well, now that you're here, might as well help me out. Grab the other end of this frame for me?

(Pause.)

Come on.

*(**SANAM** stays where she is.)*

Sanam.

SANAM. What?

ARIEL. Six years. Six years and you're still scared of bees.

SANAM. Normal people are scared of bees.

*(**ARIEL** rolls her eyes and cracks a hint of a smile.)*

ARIEL. Come on, you big baby. Wear these.

*(**ARIEL** takes off her protective veil and gloves and hands them out to **SANAM**.)*

SANAM. No, no, you need them.

ARIEL. I really don't. Here.

*(**SANAM** cautiously inches closer and takes the veil and gloves. She puts them on. **ARIEL** turns back to the hive, completely at ease.)*

Come closer. Stand over there.

(**SANAM** *stands on the other side of the hive.*)

Now hold the other end of this. Like so. It'll be a bit heavy, okay? We're going to lift it straight up. One, two – there we go.

(*They lift the inner box, containing the frame. It is covered with bees, heavy with pollen and honey.*)

Hmm.

(**SANAM** *twitches nervously.*)

Don't make any sudden movements. It's fine. They're not gonna kamikaze themselves on your account.

(*They put the box on the ground.* **ARIEL** *examines the bees in the frame.*)

SANAM. Kamikaze?

ARIEL. You know. If they sting you, they die.

SANAM. Oh, yes. Of course.

(*Pause.*)

So what's happening here exactly? What are you seeing?

ARIEL. This is interesting. They might be about to swarm.

(**SANAM** *instinctively takes a step back.*)

SANAM. Oh.

ARIEL. (*Steadying the frame.*) Not like, this second.

SANAM. Oh, okay.

How can you tell?

ARIEL. (*Like a middle-school teacher.*) Well, what do you think?

Come closer.

(**SANAM** *picks up the smoker and comes closer to look at the frame.*)

SANAM. It seems a bit full. So much honey.

ARIEL. Yeah, the frame is packed with food, but no eggs. Oh wait. Look. Queen eggs. The colony's trying to raise a new Queen.

SANAM. To leave behind, right? Because the old Queen will leave with half the colony to build a new hive.

ARIEL. *(Pleased at her student.)* Yes, exactly.

> *(Bees buzz louder.)*

Shh. Okay, okay.

> *(**ARIEL** puts the frame gently aside and starts lifting the next one for inspection.)*

I wonder what they're talking about.

When I was little, I used to swear that I understood the language of bees. That I could hear the queens when they were piping.

God, I hope they're not swarming.

SANAM. It's kind of a pain, right? You have to catch them...?

ARIEL. Yeah. The bees may have found a perfect spot for their new hive, but the people who live in that house might not be as happy.

> *(**ARIEL** keeps inspecting the hive. **SANAM** takes a second, and speaks.)*

SANAM. I – I read something yesterday that gave me an idea.

ARIEL. Yeah?

SANAM. Honey bee colonies are growing – overall – when the queens are being artificially harvested.

ARIEL. Yeah, some beekeepers do that, it's not exactly kosher.

SANAM. Yes. But that made me think – in our study – the results aren't what we wanted – but that's because the colonies weren't as affected in the last six months. The death rate had declined. That's what threw us off. The situation was actually becoming better.

ARIEL. Yeah.

SANAM. So it's possible, that the bees were becoming immune to the neonics.

ARIEL. You think?

SANAM. Maybe they're figuring it out themselves. The sixth generation of honey bees in our experiment – maybe they evolved.

ARIEL. Maybe.

SANAM. It's a possibility. I think it's worth exploring. I think it's worth...pursuing.

ARIEL. You wanna start over again?

SANAM. No, we continue.

ARIEL. I thought you'd be on to bigger and better things.

SANAM. *(Pause.)* Not when there's still work to do.

> (**ARIEL** *continues working on the hive.*)

ARIEL. How? I mean...how would we even...

SANAM. We'll find a way.

> (*A moment.* **ARIEL** *reaches out to take* **SANAM'***s hand, and squeezes it.* **ARIEL** *then turns back to her hive and lifts up the center frame.*)

So...are they going to swarm or not?

ARIEL. *(Awed and surprised.)* Shit.

SANAM. What?

ARIEL. *(This is so cool.)* Shit. This is crazy.

SANAM. What?

ARIEL. They're not swarming. They're getting rid of the old Queen.

SANAM. What?

ARIEL. Look. They've hatched a new virgin Queen. Right here. See her? In the corner.

SANAM. *(Scared of bees, hating this.)* Uh...yes?

ARIEL. And so now the worker bees are – wow, this is crazy. I can't remember the last time I saw this happening.

SANAM. What's happening?

ARIEL. The worker bees are balling the old Queen. Look. They're crowding all over her. They're cuddling her to death.

SANAM. What?

ARIEL. Their body heat will raise the temperature of the old Queen, until she dies.

SANAM. Oh, god, this is awful.

ARIEL. No, it's amazing. It's natural. It's how bees replenish and sustain themselves. I can't believe our timing. I can't believe we're getting to see this.

SANAM. You're weird.

ARIEL. Watch. Come here. This is...look.

　　　(Pause.)

She's dead.

SANAM. Ugh.

ARIEL. It's okay. She had a good life. She served this hive well, but her time is done.

　　　(A moment.)

SANAM. What happens now?

ARIEL. Can you hear the change in the piping? "The Queen is dead. Long live the Queen."

SANAM. Funny.

ARIEL. Life goes on. The old Queen wasn't viable anymore, so now they're starting over with a new one. Taking a chance on a new Queen bee. A new beginning. A new idea.

　　　(They stand there for a few moments, the sun setting behind them.)

　　　*(**SANAM** suddenly winces. She's been stung.)*

SANAM. Ow!

　　　*(**ARIEL** laughs and goes to check on her friend.)*

　　　(Lights down.)

End of Play